For Rick,
with great big Bear hugs
—J.T.

Farrar Straus Giroux Books for Young Readers
An imprint of Macmillan Publishing Group, LLC
175 Fifth Avenue, New York 10010

Copyright © 2017 by Janee Trasler
All rights reserved
Color separations by Embassy Graphics
Printed in China by RR Donnelley Asia Printing Solutions Ltd.,
Dongguan City, Guangdong Province
Designed by Roberta Pressel
First edition, 2017

1 3 5 7 9 10 8 6 4 2

mackids.com

Library of Congress Cataloging-in-Publication Data
Names: Trasler, Janee, author, illustrator.
Title: Mimi and Bear make a friend / Janee Trasler.
Description: First edition. | New York : Farrar Straus Giroux, 2017. |
    Summary: A rabbit named Mimi and her toy bear meet a new friend at the
    playground.
Identifiers: LCCN 2016034914 | ISBN 9780374303600 (hardback)
Subjects: | CYAC: Friendship—Fiction. | Playgrounds—Fiction. | Teddy
    bears—Fiction. | Rabbits—Fiction. | Animals—Fiction. | BISAC: JUVENILE
    FICTION / Toys, Dolls, Puppets. | JUVENILE FICTION / Social Issues /
    Friendship. | JUVENILE FICTION / Animals / Rabbits.
Classification: LCC PZ7.T6872 Mk 2017 | DDC [E]—dc23
LC record available at https://lccn.loc.gov/2016034914

Our books may be purchased in bulk for promotional, educational, or business use.
Please contact your local bookseller or the Macmillan Corporate and Premium Sales Department
at (800) 221-7945 ext. 5442 or by e-mail at MacmillanSpecialMarkets@macmillan.com.

Mimi and Bear
Make a Friend

Janee Trasler

FARRAR STRAUS GIROUX • New York

When Mimi and Bear
went to the park,

Mimi was the best at everything.

She was the best
mountain climber.

The best treasure hunter.

The best downhill skier.

And she was definitely
the best trapeze artist.

But one day, when Mimi and Bear got to the park,

somebody was already there.

Now Mimi was NOT the best mountain climber.

Somebody was better.

She was not the best treasure hunter or downhill skier, either.

Somebody was better.

Mimi was not even the best
trapeze artist anymore.

Somebody . . .

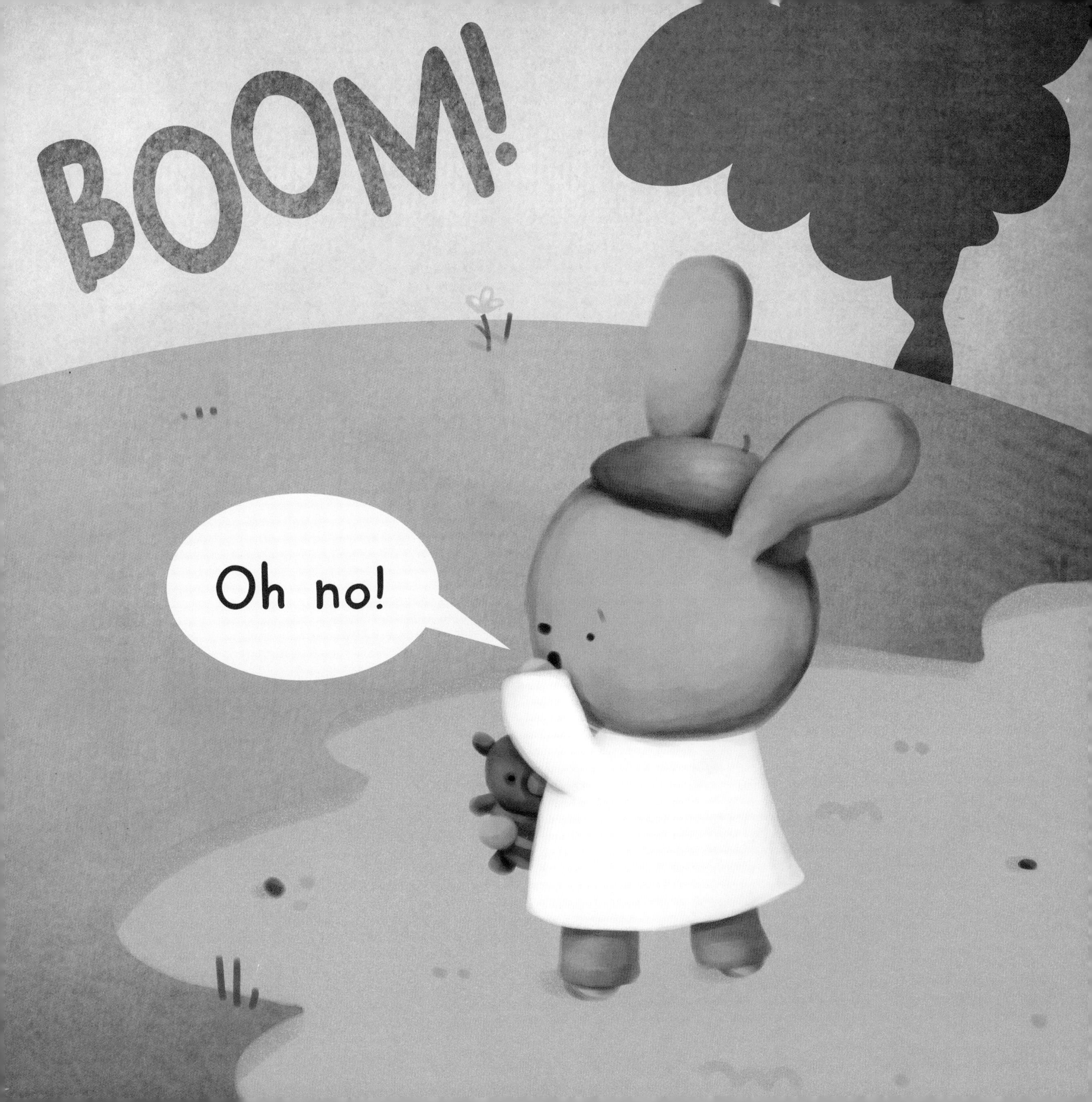
BOOM!
Oh no!

Mimi may not have
been the best at
everything,

but she was definitely
a good friend.

Everybody thought so.